Winter

Nicola Baxter

Illustrated by Kim Woolley

 CHILDRENS PRESS ®

A Division of Grolier Publishing
New York ● London ● Hong Kong ● Sydney
Danbury, Connecticut

During the autumn, the days grow shorter and the weather gets colder.
Slowly winter arrives.

Now try this...
Do you think the photograph on the next page was taken in the autumn or the winter?
Can you be really sure?

The winter sun is not very hot.
We need to wear warm clothes
when it is cold outside.

Now try this...
Some people put their summer clothes away when the
weather gets colder. Which of these clothes might
you wear in the winter?

Running and playing keeps you warm too.
But you can tell that it is cold if you can
"see" your breath.

Try this later...
On a cold day, blow on to the window pane.
The cold glass will turn your breath
into tiny drops of water.
The same thing happens to your breath
in the air outdoors on a very cold day.

Sometimes it is so cold outside that water freezes and turns into ice. Putting salt on roads and paths helps stop people from slipping.

When it is cold, rain is frozen
as it falls from the clouds.
It may fall as little lumps of ice,
called sleet, or as snowflakes.

Try this later...

Under a microscope, all snowflakes have
six sides and each one is different.
Draw around a plate on white paper
and cut out the circle.
Ask a grown-up to help you follow these
steps to make your own snowflake.

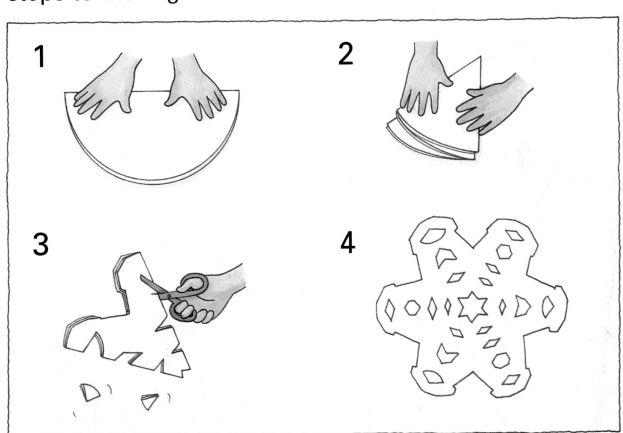

If the weather is very cold, the ground may be covered with snow all winter.

Some sports and games can be played only when it is very cold.

When you have been outside
in the cold, hot food and drinks
taste good and warm you up.

Farmers need to feed their animals extra food to keep them going through the winter.

It is sometimes hard for birds and other animals to find food.
When ponds and puddles are frozen, it is difficult to find water to drink too.

Try this later...

In winter, put some food and fresh water in
a safe place on your windowsill or in a bird feeder.
Watch quietly to see which birds visit it.

During winter celebrations, candles and
lights cheer up the cold, dark days
and remind people that the winter
can be a time of new beginnings too.

For many people, the beginning of a new year is celebrated in the winter.

Try this later...
Ask a grown-up to help you make
a calendar of the year.
Draw or cut out pictures for each month
and be sure to mark the times that
are special to you each year.

Winter seems to last a long time.
But even before winter is over,
the first signs of spring can be seen.

Index

© 1996 Franklin Watts

First American Edition 1996 by
Children's Press
A Division of Grolier Publishing
Sherman Turnpike
Danbury, Connecticut 06816

Printed in Malaysia

Library of Congress Cataloging-in-Publication Data
Baxter, Nicola.
    Winter / Nicola Baxter.
        p. cm. - (Toppers)
    Includes index.
    Summary: A simple discussion of various facets of winter, including cold weather and snow, warm clothing and foods, and winter holidays.
    ISBN 0-531-09277-4 (lib. bdg.)
    ISBN 0-516-26088-X (pbk.)
    1. Winter – Juvenile literature.
    [1. Winter.].] I. Title. II. Series: Baxter, Nicola, Toppers.
    QB637.8. B39 1996   95-50049
    508–dc20   CIP AC

Editor: Sarah Ridley
Designer; Kirstie Billingham
Picture researcher: Sarah Moule

Acknowledgments: the publishers would like to thank Carol Olivier and Kenmont Primary School for their help with the cover for this book.

Photographs: Bubbles 5, 6; Bruce Coleman Ltd 9, 23; James Davis Travel Photography 13; Robert Harding Picture Library 10; Natural History Photographic Agency 3, 16; Oxford Scientific Films 15; Trip 18, 21.